Digby
Helps at the Zoo

by
Alan Aburrow-Newman

Illustrated by
Gill Guile

Brimax · Newmarket · England

It was a hot, sunny day. Digby was helping to build a new playground for the gorillas at the zoo. It had to be strong, because the gorillas had broken the last one. The new one had stronger poles for climbing on, thicker rope for swinging from and tougher nets for jumping into.

The gorillas were pleased with their new playground. Just to make sure that Digby had made a good job of everything, they decided to give it their own special test. Wallop, the biggest gorilla, jumped up and down on the bridge. Another gorilla did a forward roll down the slide. Five others tugged at the same knotted rope. They all crashed and banged, but nothing was broken. Digby was very pleased.

"No matter how hard they try, I don't think the gorillas will wreck this playground," he said.

Digby noticed Ernie and Edna the hippos in the next paddock. They looked very grumpy. They were standing in a dirty pit, puffing and snorting, and blowing dust into the air. Larry, the head keeper, was sitting on the fence spraying them with water from a hose.

"Oh dear," said Digby. "Are you going to give them a bath?"
Larry looked hot and bothered, too.
"No, I'm just trying to cool them down," he said. "They are too hot, and the sun has dried up the mud in their hollow."
"Well, if Ernie and Edna get much hotter, they will shrivel up like giant raisins!" said Digby.
"They need lots of mud to cool down in," said Larry.

"Leave this to me," said Digby. "Come on, Big Bill," said Digby to his driver.
"Let's visit the sea-lions."

It was feeding time at the sea-lions' pool. Their keeper was throwing them fish to eat and a crowd of children was cheering as the sea-lions leaped out of the water.

"The sea-lions will be too busy to notice what I'm doing," said Digby.
"What are you planning?" asked Big Bill. "I hope you're not going to
get us into trouble."
"I thought we could *borrow* some of the sea-lions' water, and use it to
make a muddy pond for the hippos," said Digby.
"What a good idea!" said Big Bill excitedly. "But how are we going to
get the water back to the hippo paddock?"
"That's easy," said Digby.

Digby plunged his front bucket into the sea-lions' pool, and scooped
up enough water to fill twenty bath-tubs. He was just about to go
back to the hippo paddock when a sea-lion peered over the edge of
the bucket.

"Oh dear! I've kidnapped a sea-lion," chuckled Digby. "You had better get out of there, unless you want to share a mud-hole with two hippos!" The sea-lion leaped out of the bucket, and dived back into his pool.

When he arrived back at the hippos' paddock, Digby dumped the water with such a splash, that it washed Larry off the fence. Ernie and Edna cheered up when they saw the water, but it still wasn't mud. They wanted mud as gooey as a double-thick milkshake, so they could roll around until they looked like two chocolate hippos.

"I'll show you how to make mud!" said Digby.

Making mud was the best thing about being a digger. After a few minutes of churning and turning, the water had become a lovely deep, sticky mud that almost covered Digby's wheels.

"There you are," said Digby to Ernie and Edna, as he finally backed out of the pit. "First class mud; smooth and cool, and not a single lump!"

Ernie and Edna very slowly walked into the cool, chocolate-brown goo. They sank down in it until all that could be seen was their sleepy eyes and blissful smiles.

"Hmm," said Digby. "I wouldn't mind being a hippo myself."
Feeling very pleased with themselves, Digby and Big Bill began to head
back to the garage. Suddenly Larry, who was still very wet, signalled for
Digby to stop.

"Will you give me a ride to the giraffes' enclosure?" Larry asked. "Patches has a problem."

When they arrived, Digby could see that Patches really *did* have a problem. For a giraffe, a problem couldn't get much bigger, or longer, than a stiff neck!

Because Patches couldn't reach down to his food, he hadn't been able to eat all day. Kevin, his keeper, was trying to feed Patches by throwing fruit and vegetables for him to catch in his mouth. Kevin wasn't very good at throwing and Patches wasn't very good at catching. All they had managed to do was wedge a melon between Patches' horns!

"I can help," said Digby. "If you load Patches' dinner into my bucket,
I can lift it up to him."
Larry, Big Bill and Kevin filled Digby's bucket with fruit and vegetables,
a bale of hay and a big tub of water.

"Here comes dinner!" called Digby to Patches, and he stretched up as high as he could, so Patches could eat without bending down.

Patches couldn't decide what to eat first, so he ate a big, juicy apple while he thought about it. Eventually he decided to eat the carrots first, as he liked carrots more than anything!

After a long day standing up - and after such a fine supper, too - Patches wished that he could lay down to sleep. Then Digby started to yawn as well. After such a busy day, he could hardly keep his eyes open. Big Bill piled a huge feather pillow into Digby's bucket and lifted it up for Patches to rest his head on. Then, switching off Digby's engine, Big Bill crept away.

Soon Patches and Digby were both fast asleep.